Contents:

The Wobbly Hat of Duke Toggleton

When Duke Toggleton bought a hat

And placed it on his head,

It somehow managed to fall off

And started to unthread.

Duke Toggleton was furious;

Yelled for his money back.

But the man who'd sold it said:

"No refunds on the wobble hat!

It's written in the small print,

Oh, didn't you see?

And if you drop it two more times

It's mine again for free!"

The Duke did not like this

But frugal as he was,

He took a tightrope class

To gain some balance for the cause.

"I won't drop this hat and waste

The money that I spent!"

He said as from his wallet paid

The tightrope teaching gent.

He practiced and he practised

Until confident and sure

That he could wear his wobble hat

And know it was secure.

Suddenly a violent wind

Came rattling through the town,

And Toggleton tried hard

But couldn't stop it falling down.

If he let it fall again

He'd lose it to the seller.

Maybe, he thought, I will give it

To another feller.

Just then, across the canyon

There came a scary scream;

A mother's pram was rolling down

The hill to the ravine.

Fortunately a bridge

Was being built over the drop;

Unfortunately the weather meant

Production had to stop.

A rope was all there was

To the far-off other side;

Duke Toggleton put on his hat

And swallowed down his pride.

He stepped onto the tightrope,

(Which wasn't tight at all)

Trying not to think of if he slipped

How far that he would fall.

A gust of wind came at him

Making him buckle and bend;

Duke Toggleton was wobbling

As he leapt for the far end.

The baby in the pram

Now came tumbling off the edge.

Duke with his left arm grabbed the kid

His right grasping the ledge.

That day he was a hero;

He'd saved the woman's son.

The Duke was also quite relieved

That shoddy wobbly hat was gone.

The Crocodile

One day there was a crocodile in my loo

I wasn't sure what to do;

Call the police or fire brigade?

I told it to go, but it stayed.

One day there was a crocodile in my loo

It looked as if it had the flu.

I know that I could never go

With Crocodile down below.

One day there was a crocodile in my loo

My brother thought it wasn't true.

I wish this crocodile would leave

Then I'd feel most relieved.

One day there was a crocodile in my loo

It had bought a friend along too!

Was it a fish? Or was it an eel?

I wasn't sure how to feel.

One day the crocodile was gone!

I asked my Mum what she had done.

She said she'd pulled the lever down;

The toilet smells much nicer now.

Dragons Vs Pirates

"How do we keep our economy stable?"

The dragon's discussed around the table.

The problem was that they needed more gold,

Not to spend, but to behold,

And sit upon and throw around,

But no more gold there could be found.

They'd searched the mountains and the mines,

They'd drawn up maps and followed signs,

They'd burned down towns and planes in flight,

And stole from poor and rich alike.

Where was the more? They needed more!

Perhaps they should have looked offshore…

Where mast set high and rigging taut

A brood of pirates had just caught

Sight of a ship that had more gold

Than the whole earth could surely hold!

With swish of sword and crack of gun

The pirates had two ships, not one.

They'd become richer in one day

Than all those dragons, far away.

Or not so far as so you've guessed;

Dragons had set out on their quest.

Not to land of rock and stone

But to the pirate's ocean home.

"Well I says, arrrr!" and "Yarrr! says I."

"There be beasties in the sky!"

As pirates picked out weapons for battle

The dragons hissed and spoke with a rattle.

"Give us the treasure or else, good chum"

"Or we'll burn you up, like skanky scum!"

The pirates reply

Was a "Nay says I!"

"We'll never agree,

To the death it be!"

As they shouted the sky turned black

And rain poured off the beasties backs

Extinguishing their fiery flame,

And as they cursed, the pirates came

To tie them up with ropes of steel

All round the soggy battlefield.

The dragons responded super quick;

They put their weight on one big ship

And down it sank to the depths below,

The angry pirates had a go:

"You idiots! That's all the gold!

I hope you swim, you wormy trolls!"

"Oh," said dragons, all as one,

"Our plan seems to have gone all wrong."

They then began to fly away

But Captain Pirate shouted "Stay!"

The puzzled dragons whirled around;

The rain stopped dead and sun came out.

"If we want this buried treasure,

We're going to have to work together!"

The Captain's plan he soon did tell

Which somehow went down really well.

And so there was the strangest sight:

A pirate-riding-dragon flight.

Towards the sea they breathed their fire

And underneath a heat so dire,

The ocean boiled to the floor

Where gold shined brighter than before.

The pirates gathered all they could,

(The dragon's claws were no good)

Then they shared their sweet delight,

And all became firm friends that night.

Harry's Headphones

Harry had his headphones on;
He couldn't hear a thing.
He didn't hear the buzzing bee
Threatening to sting.

Harry didn't hear the sound
Of Mum call him for dinner.
Harry had his headphones on
And he felt like a winner.

Harry didn't hear the bell;
His music made him grin.
He didn't hear his teacher moaning
When later he got in.

Harry's headphones were so loud

It made some people glare.

For some his music was a sound

They simply couldn't bear.

Harry had his headphones on

And didn't hear the roar

Of a car that moved so fast

And smashed him to the core.

Harry has his headphones on;

Quietly in bed.

And when people come nearby

He takes them off his head.

Antler Facts

Ok, I'm growing antlers.

Is this a good idea?

I don't want to be a tree,

Just a normal male deer.

I suppose I had it coming;

It happened to my brother.

But his came off last winter

And he went crying to mother.

She told him they'll grow back,

Reach their highest height in August

And fall off again in January

Or later if they must.

My uncle has one good one,

But the other on his right

Is stunted and quite twisted,

A really weird sight.

He had an awful injury

To his left-sided leg,

And it went right up and altered

The right-hand side of his head.

My grandfather has antlers

That get smaller every summer.

I hope that mine get bigger,

Or else that would be a bummer.

There are a lot of things about

Deer antlers I don't know,

And though I'm not a tree I hope

My branch-like antlers grow.

I don't want to be a bushel

Or a piece of shrubbery

And I'll scratch my antlers against

Any deer-mocking tree!

I say, I say, I say!

I say, I say, I say!

What an awful racket.

It made my monocle fall off;

I had to stoop to catch it.

If those naughty boys don't stop

I'll smack them with my cane.

After if they don't shut up

I'll hit them once again.

I say, I say, I say!

What an awful smell.

It made me shudder and my top hat

Toppled down a well.

If those naughty boys don't wash

I'll hit them with my cane.

After if they shower not

I'll give them some more pain.

I say, I say, I say!

What an awful sight.

It made me drop my brolly

And it flew off like a kite.

It's those naughty boys again

Getting in my way.

It's time to get the cane out

As they begin to say…

We say, we say, we say!

It's that mean old guy.

Should we run away before

He beats us 'til we die?

I know let's just take his stick

That he uses to walk.

Then he cannot hit us;

And we can play and talk.

I say, I say, I say!

Those scoundrels stole my cane!

How dare they do this thing to me;

An old man in pain.

My back is twisted because

When I was young and quick,

I tried too hard to twist away

From my teacher's stick.

Beard

The day I turned thirteen

There came shooting out my face,

A tough and tangled thicket

That felt truly out of place.

So I hacked at it with shears

Until I had cut free,

But before the sun was up

It grew back branches like a tree.

A hacksaw was needed

And although it took all day,

By evening I had managed

To get most out of the way.

The third morning I was lost

In a forest or a wood.

I tried to find a way out

But didn't think I could.

The next day I met a guy

Who was completely bald.

He said "Brother, I know how you're feeling,

If the truth be told.

Take this balding cream here,

And spread it on your chin.

Then your beard will come right off

So you can put it in the bin."

I did just as directed

And found that he was right!

Now I had a hairless chin,

An amazing sight!

Although a few years later,

When I couldn't grow a 'tash,

I thought back to my thicket

As if that was greener grass.

Monkey Diarrhoea

Monkey's banana was not yet ripe,

And tasted too solid and sour.

But monkey took another bite;

Too impatient to wait for the ripening hour.

Uncle advised: "If you just pause,

Time will release its flavour!"

What does uncle know about nature's laws?

I'm hungry, do me a favour!

Monkey's tub was not yet full,

And yellow from yesterday's splash.

But cleaning out the water's dull!

It takes too long to have a bath.

"You're too impatient!" Uncle said.

"If you don't wash you'll stink!"

I'm tired I think I'll go to bed.

Sleeping is patient, don't you think?

Monkey's morning had not yet come,

But sleep was boring too.

He thought he would get something done

And went to the monkey loo.

Too tired to notice his body was smelly;

From ants he could not defend.

The unripe banana inside his belly

Caused problems at the other end.

Before he knew it the ants had attacked,

So monkey shouted for help.

And uncles arm smothered and smacked

To free the impatient whelp.

The monkey's banana was not yet ripe;

The taste was sour and viscous.

So monkey *waited* to take a bite

And when he did it tasted delicious.

Cherries

King Henry ate a cherry

On a ferry in the sun,

But that very afternoon he found

The cherries had all gone.

So he called to all his porters

And his sorters down the line,

And said "I'll have you caught

If you sought cherry's 'cause they're mine!"

No-one would admit they had

The wit to nick the fruit,

But they were a bit unfit

And had each stolen a shoot.

An embarrassed ferryman

Had found a bushel in the forest,

And put cherries in a can

For a florist that he cherished.

But the florist, (not impressed

With the cherries from the forest)

Had confessed that she was leaving

For her parents off in Paris.

The ferryman, consoled

By the whole bushel in a bowl,

Before duties from his beauties

Called him to his ferry goal.

Henry who was not merry;

Without cherries felt a wreck.

Before he cheered as there appeared

A plate of berries on the deck.

Rhythm and Beat

I tried to play the violin,

But man, it hurt my ears.

I tinkered on the keyboards,

And that confirmed my fears.

I could not hear the difference

Between the notes at all,

So when they got me a guitar,

I swapped it for a ball.

I really do love music,

I wish it came with ease,

But I will never join the band

With ears as bad as these.

Then one day I was shopping,

And feeling rather glum,

When out the corner of my eye

I spotted a small drum.

Feeling quite frustrated,

I gave it a big whack,

Until a passer-by proclaimed,

"I think you've got the knack!"

So that day I bought it,

And drummed the whole way home;

Joined a band of people who

All knew their music tones.

I don't know what they're playing,

I'm sure it is a treat,

Whatever it is, it comes alive

With my rhythm and beat!

The Goat and the Ox and the Cow

Twenty pirates sat in a boat

Along with an ox and a cow and a goat.

Goat was quite a scholarly fellow.

Ox's teeth were cracked and yellow.

Cow was plump and round and fat.

The pirates plotted where they sat.

"Let's cook the cow, she looks tasty,

That old goat is pale and pasty,

And as for Ox, he looks the worst,

We'll eat him last, but fatty first."

Goat thought very hard that day,

Deciding they should get away.

"Hey Ox," he muttered, "can you swim?"

"Why, yes!" the ox replied to him.

"Let's escape then, you and me

Cow will be just fine, you'll see!"

Ox replied he would not go

And leave their friend behind, alone.

"Every time the clock tick-tocks

We're losing time, you stubborn ox!

Fine, we'll bring along the cow,

I only wish that I knew how..."

As pirates sharpened up their knives

There came a mooing from behind.

Cow was swimming, out the boat;

Beckoning to the old goat.

"Up on my back now, and be quick!

Staying would be very thick."

For land the animals then set,

(Goat trying not to get wet)

"We got you out!" the goat then cheered,

But Cow had never really feared:

"Don't you understand my friend?

Pirates couldn't be my end.

Wasn't me afraid of water,

Thinking life was getting shorter.

I can swim; Ox can too,

We we're trying to rescue you!"

Waiting for Pizza

We waited for pizza to arrive,

We ordered it at five past five.

It would help us all survive

If the pizza should arrive.

Our fridge is empty, never full.

Cupboard deserted, damp and dull.

I search for scraps like a sea-gull,

But wouldn't if our fridge was full.

I hope they find the right address,

Our house is like a hive or nest,

Delivery boy put to the test,

He'll pass if he finds our address.

I hear our stomachs rumbling,

Our patience slowly crumbling,

Sustenance absence humbling

At sound of stomachs rumbling.

Maybe we should have planned for this;

Got all the shopping on the list.

Surely life would just be bliss

If only we had planned for this.

Finally a knock upon the door:

The pizza man that we adore!

Take all our change and even more

Now our pizza's through the door.

No pineapple upon the top,

Are you joking? No I'm not.

Take it to the bin to drop,

We need pineapple on the top.

Pizza should come in a tick and a tock,

We ordered it at 6 o'clock,

The bin is one big pizza block,

Pizza perfection in a tick-tock.

The Letter

I'm waiting for the mailman

To deliver me my post,

Whilst I turn the kettle on

And spread butter on my toast.

An important letter should

Come through the door quite soon,

And I really do not want it read

By any old buffoon.

So I'll pour a bit more water

In the kettle now to boil,

And I'll unwrap some more bread

From its packaging of foil.

Finally a knock upon the door,

This must be my letter!

But when I ask the postie says

He's got me something better.

A box of something somehow has

My name upon the sides,

I am annoyed but curious

And that's what overrides.

It's an alarm clock with a little

Note onto it tacked,

"Work starts at 9 o'clock mate,

Stop waiting to be sacked."

I didn't get my letter;

Had to accept my loss,

And went to work to make some toast

And coffee for my boss.

Back to School

First day back at school,

No more chilling playing pool.

No more running round in town;

Lego bricks are now put down.

I can't eat any more bugs,

Or get friction burn on rugs.

Have to wear a uniform;

Sew up tatty trousers torn.

Football only now at break,

For which I can't really wait.

At least there's stuff I'll learn,

But it's getting hard this term.

If I get stuck I'll ask;

They are very bright, my class.

Not exactly locked and barred,

But being a teacher's hard!

The Scarecrow

Gerald sat upon a horse

Looking 'cross the vale,

When a scarecrow caught his eye,

And Gerald's face grew pale.

"What is now this hideousness

That wrecks my perfect view?"

And so the man removed it,

Before chopping it into two.

Gerald's horse awoke next day,

And turned his solemn gaze

Upon the hazy vale where on

The grass he liked to graze.

But to his utter disbelief

A swarm of birds had sat,

Upon the very piece of ground

That was his, in fact!

This simply would not do,

So he woke his portly master,

To tell him of the ruined view

And ugly bird disaster.

Gerold had a bright idea,

(That he'd had before)

Of hammering a giant scarecrow

To the valley floor.

"That takes care of that!" he chortled,

As they went to sleep,

But on the morrow

This sad little tale did repeat.

Bladder

Yes, I certainly agree

That right now I need a wee.

My bladder's like a big beach ball,

I can't go now though, not at all.

Why? Let me make this clear,

For these reasons listed here:

It's my cue in the school play

I must be on without delay.

There is pressure, certainly,

It's building up, can't you all see?

I'm in a meeting that is long,

My boss's speech goes on and on.

This part is crucial, aimed at me,

Should I just wee here quietly?

I'm in a roller-coaster queue,

I'll lose my place, it's sad but true!

I'm on a boat, I'm in a lift,

My costume is too tight and stiff.

For these and a thousand more

I cannot go now and what's more,

I had a big lunch so quite soon,

All that food will want out too!

The End

Printed in Great Britain
by Amazon